Jane Yolen

ILLUSTRATED BY
Chris Sheban

DESIGNED BY Rita Marshall

WHAT TO DO WITH A BOX

CREATIVE ✺ EDITIONS

FRAGILE

Text copyright © 2016 by Jane Yolen   Illustrations copyright © 2016 by Chris Sheban

Edited by Kate Riggs   Published in 2016 by Creative Editions   P.O. Box 227, Mankato, MN 56002 USA

Creative Editions is an imprint of The Creative Company   www.thecreativecompany.us

Library of Congress Cataloging-in-Publication Data

Yolen, Jane. What to do with a box / by Jane Yolen; illustrated by Chris Sheban.

Summary: Jane Yolen poetically reminds young readers that a simple box can be a child's most
imaginative plaything as artist Chris Sheban illustrates its myriad and magical uses.

ISBN 978-1-56846-289-9   [1. Stories in rhyme. 2. Boxes-Fiction. 3. Imagination-Fiction. 4. Play-Fiction.]

I. Sheban, Chris, illustrator. II. Title.   PZ8.3.Y76Wg 2016   [E]-dc23   2015008269

9 8 7 6 5 4 3

A BOX! A BOX IS A STRANGE DEVICE.

You can open it once.

You can open it
twice.

You can climb inside
and there read a
book.
It can be
a library,

PALACE,

OR NOOK.

You can lock the door
with a magical
key,

INVITE
YOUR DOLLS
TO COME IN FOR
TEA.

YOU CAN PAINT
A LANDSCAPE
WITH SUN,

OR CRAYON
AN EGRET
THAT'S FLYING
RIGHT BY.

Or paint a blue river
and very
green trees.
(You can borrow a
fan
just to make a small
breeze.)

You can drive
in that box
all around a dirt track.

You can sail
in that box
off to Paris
and back.

A BOX! A BOX
IS A WONDER
INDEED.
THE ONLY
SUCH MAGIC
THAT YOU'LL
EVER NEED.

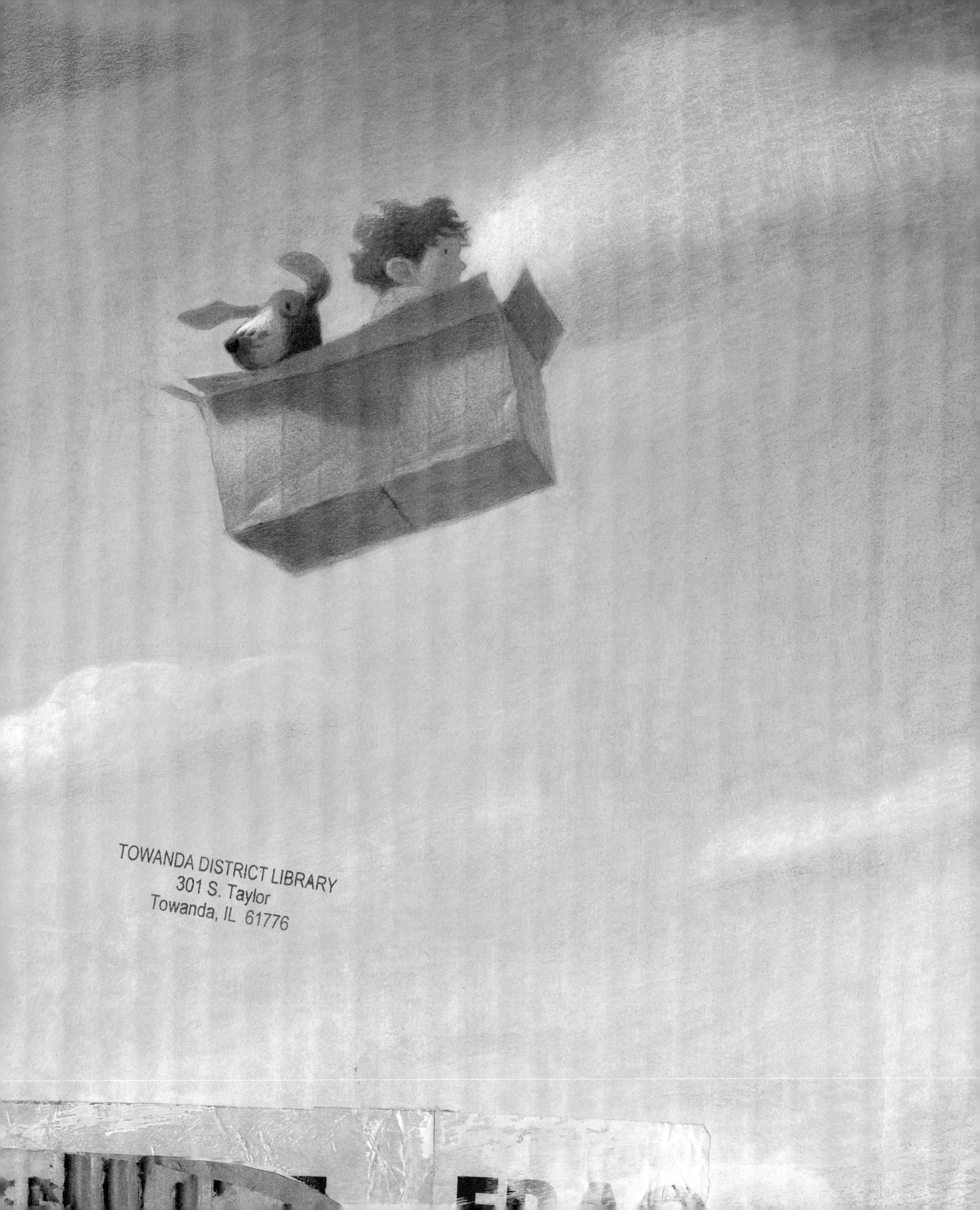

So come for a visit
right now.
Right this day!
I've got a grand
box
just so we two can
play.

Corrugated
Recycles

23X19X12

MICHIGAN BOX COMPANY
BOX CERTIFICATE
THIS
SINGLEWALL
BOX MEETS ALL CONSTRUCTION
REQUIREMENTS OF APPLICABLE
FREIGHT CLASSIFICATION
EDGE CRUSH
TEST (ECT)   32
SIZE LIMIT   75   LBS/IN
GROSS WT LT   65   INCHES
DETROIT, MICHIGAN